This book is dedicated to my Starr, who found me and showed me through her own happiness that I could truly be myself, and that was enough for me to Shine. Thank you, Roxanne, for helping me find the courage to chase my dream.

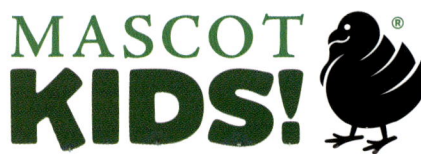

www.mascotbooks.com

Starr's Wonderful Discovery

©2021 Trey Jefferies. All Rights Reserved. No part of this publication may be reproduced, stored in a retrieval system or transmitted in any form by any means electronic, mechanical, or photocopying, recording or otherwise without the permission of the author.

For more information, please contact:
Mascot Books
620 Herndon Parkway, Suite 320
Herndon, VA 20170
info@mascotbooks.com

Library of Congress Control Number: 2021910946

CPSIA Code: PRT0921A
ISBN-13: 978-1-64543-953-0

Printed in the United States

Starr's Wonderful Discovery

Trey Jefferies

Illustrated by Andrés Cornejo

Once upon a time, in a beautiful, lush, green, bamboo forest, there lived a group of pandas. All of the pandas were happy, and they lived together peacefully.

One of the pandas was a beautiful panda named Starr. Starr was loved by everyone. She had soft, lovely fur. The black on her fur sparkled like the night sky, and the white on her fur glittered like diamonds in fresh snow. Starr was always rolling and playing in the forest, laughing and joking with her friends, and loving and caring for the other pandas.

Starr also did something special: she sang. Starr sang everywhere she went. She loved to sing, and she had a beautiful voice. Starr sang everything: songs she heard in the mountains, and even songs she made up herself!

Starr especially loved singing in the mornings to greet the day. She would walk through the bamboo forest early in the morning, singing her made-up tunes softly as the rest of the pandas woke up. This was Starr's gift to them: helping the other pandas start their days.

One morning, Starr woke up early to welcome the new day. The clouds were especially low and beautiful that day, and Starr felt like she was walking right through them, imagining she was in heaven. This made Starr happy, and she started to sing. As she began to sing, the clouds began to lift, floating up the mountain. Wanting to stay in the cloud as long as possible, Starr started following the cloud up the mountain.

Higher and higher she went, climbing up through the bamboo forest following the clouds and singing her song. As Starr got closer to the top, she began to hear another voice singing. She stopped for a moment to listen to its beautiful song. Suddenly, she realized...the voice belonged to another panda!

I'm the only panda in the forest who likes to sing, thought Starr. *I wonder who that charming voice belongs to!* Starr was curious, so she followed the voice, which was coming from higher up the mountain. As she climbed higher, the voice got louder and closer. It was soft but deep, and Starr was captivated by its melody.

Starr climbed higher and higher, and eventually came to a clearing in the bamboo. The clouds blocked her view, but Starr could still make out the shape of a large panda on the other side of the clearing—the source of the song! Starr noticed that the other panda was big and strong, but his voice was soft and gentle. As his song came to a pause, the panda started another, and Starr began to sing along.

Startled by the sound of her voice, the other panda stopped singing and spun around, looking right at Starr. "Who are you? What are you doing up here?" the other panda asked, surprised to hear another panda in the clearing.

Starr walked out of the clouds and into the clearing. "Don't stop singing. It was beautiful! My name is Starr, and I love to sing, too," she explained.

"But…why are you up here? I don't usually see anyone else up here," replied the other panda.

"I was following the cloud up from the valley when I heard your voice. It was so beautiful that I had to see who was singing," Starr said with a smile. "What's your name?"

"My name is Shine," answered the other panda. "I live here alone." Shine turned away, embarrassed.

Starr moved closer to Shine. "Please sing some more. I'd love to sing with you," she pleaded.

Shine stayed quiet and moved away from Starr, looking uncomfortable. Starr moved closer to him still.

"I'm sorry that I interrupted you, but I've never heard another panda sing before. Please sing some more?" Starr pleaded again.

"I don't sing in front of anyone," Shine said, beginning to tear up. "The other pandas make fun of me when I sing."

Starr felt sad for Shine. She wondered why anyone would make fun of someone with such a charming voice. "But why? Why would anyone make fun of you?" Starr questioned.

Head hanging low, with tears in his eyes, Shine answered, "I'm a boy panda, and everyone says that I'm supposed to be big and strong. I'm not supposed to sing." As he spoke, his voice cracked with embarrassment and hurt.

Starr moved closer to Shine and put her paw on his shoulder, comforting him.

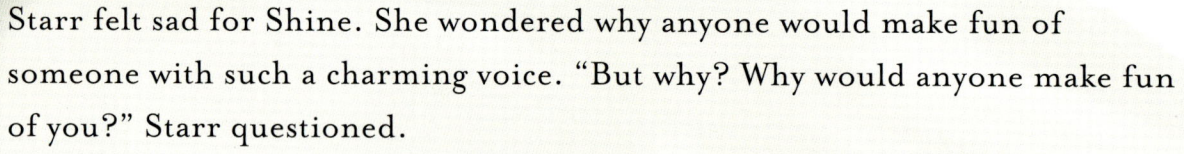

"I love to sing, so I came up here to do it where no one can make fun of me."
Shine was upset as he remembered the jokes other pandas made about him.

Starr felt bad for Shine, and she wanted to make him happy. She put her arm around him and said, "Why don't we sing together, since we both love to sing? It'll be fun!"

Shine stuttered back, "I-I d-d-don't sing in fr-front of people."

"How about we just sing our names? I'll start by singing my name, and then you can sing yours," Starr suggested. "I'll go first. Starrrr…"

Shine said nothing, so she sang it again. "Starrrr…"

This time, Shine sang softly back. *"SHINE..."*

Starr sang again, this time louder. *"STARRR..."*

Shine lifted his head and sang in his deep, charming voice, *"SHIIINE..."*

And so, the two pandas began to sing together: "STARRRR!" "SHIIIINE!"

Their voices complemented each other perfectly. Starr and Shine began to circle each other, both of them smiling.

"STARRR...SHIIIINE...STARRR...SHIIIINE...STARRR...SHIIIINE..."

Each time the pandas sang their names, they grew happier and happier. They began to harmonize, their voices blending together in song.

As they sang, Starr began to slowly walk down the mountain. Shine was so happy to be singing with another panda that he started walking with her. He didn't even notice they were going down the mountain!

"STARRR...SHIIIINE...STARRR...SHIIIINE...STARRR...SHIIIINE..."

As their voices echoed down into the forest below, Starr and Shine moved further and further down the mountain. Their song began to reach the other pandas, who were just waking up. They listened with joy to the song that was the perfect blend of beauty and strength.

"STARRR...SHIIIINE...STARRR...SHIIIINE...STARRR...SHIIIINE..."

As Starr and Shine neared the valley, all of the other pandas, now awake, came running up the mountain to find out where the amazing chorus they were hearing was coming from. They were all surprised when they saw Starr and this new panda walking together and singing on their way down the path.

Starr and Shine continued to sing, looking deep into each other's eyes as they walked into the bottom of the valley. Shine didn't even notice the other pandas at first, because he was so caught up in the song.

Starr slowly brought Shine to the center of the panda forest, the two of them singing the whole way.

"STARRR...SHIIIINE...STARRR...SHIIIINEE...STARRR...SHIIIINE..."

All the other pandas surrounded them, listening happily. It was clear that these two singing pandas, Starr and Shine, were meant to be friends. The way their voices blended together, the way their names went together, and the way they looked into each other's eyes …everything about the pair was magical!

"STARRR...SHIIIINE...STARRR...SHIIIINE...STARRR...SHIIIINE..."

As Shine sang with Starr, he noticed...no one was making fun of him!

Starr had discovered Shine, and Shine had found a home.

From that day on, Starr and Shine greeted each day together, walking through the bamboo forest singing as the sun rose each morning.

"STARRR...SHIIIINE...STARRR...SHIIIINE...STARRR...SHIIIINE..."

THE END

About the Author

Trey Jefferies is a fourth-generation native and resident of Jacksonville, Florida. He is the proud father of four children—sons Rider and Steele and daughters Madison and Sydney—and an American bulldog, Toby. Trey is a successful entrepreneur with a passion for writing and communicating. He finds that pursuing his love of writing enables him to excel in other aspects of life.

Trey's passion for writing began in seventh grade at the Assumption School in Jacksonville, where he was first encouraged to write by his English teacher, Marianne Buerkle. Since then, Trey has been published in *Jacksonville Mom* and creates content for his own blog, *The Simple Cowboy*. Trey believes in the importance of following your passion, has taught his children to do the same, and strives to prove daily that's where the magic is found.